JUGGLING THE JITTERS

By Deborah Fannie Miller

Illustrated by Danielle Bazin

Today, Papa kissed me good morning. I had a good morning and a great day, too.

Tonight, Papa said, "Go to sleep now, Jacob," and kissed me "Good night."

I am not having a good night.

I'm too excited to sleep.
Tomorrow, I'm going to my friend
Kathleen's birthday party.

I hope Kathleen likes my present.
Will I make new friends?
Will I get a balloon?
There is so much to think about!

"Lights out," Papa says and leaves me alone with all my thoughts.

"Jacob," Papa calls from down the hall,
"stop talking and go to bed now."

"Yikes!" say the Jitters.
"Yikes!" say I.

"Jacob," Papa calls even louder, "please stop talking — it's way past your bedtime."

I jump up. The Jitters jump up too and turn the lights back on.

Now four Jitters are jumping on my bed.

Papa calls from downstairs, "Jacob, did you just turn those lights back on?"

I jump up again and turn the lights off fast.

"Yikes!" say the Jitters.
"Yikes!" say I.

"Jacob, stop talking and
GO TO BED, PLEASE,"
Papa calls again.

Now eight Jitters are
jumping on my bed.

Maybe Kathleen won't like my present?
Maybe I won't make friends?
Maybe I won't get a balloon?

I close my eyes to block those *maybe-mumblies*.

When I open my eyes, twelve Jitters are jumping on my bed! Twelve Jitters are messing with my head.

"Yikes!" say the Jitters.
"Yikes!" say I.

What if Kathleen doesn't like presents?
What if no one wants to play?
What if my balloon pops?

I shut my ears to stop those *what-if-iffers*.

I turn my back on those jittering Jitters.

When I turn around, my room is jammed full
of jumping, jabbering Jitters.

There is no room for me in my bed.

There is no room for me in my room.

There is no room for me in my head!

It is filled with jerky jolts of jittering Jitters.

I run into the closet.
I shut the door. I close
my eyes. I shut my ears,
but my breathing is all
jittery. It is jumping in
and jumping out,
fast, fast, fast!

JUST
STOP!

The closet door opens.
Strong arms hug me.
Kisses warm the top
of my head.

Papa carries me
back to bed.

Papa brushes the hair out of my eyes.
"You're juggling the Jitters, aren't you?"
"Yes," I say.
"I get jittery too," Papa says.

"Yikes!" say the Jitters, but
we aren't listening.

"You know, you don't have to
juggle the Jitters." Papa smiles.
"I don't?" I say. The Jitters stop jittering.
"Do you want to tell me about your
jitters?" Papa asks.

I tell Papa all about the *maybe-mumblies*
and the *what-if-iffers*.
He listens and then he hugs me.

"Everyone gets the Jitters sometimes. But, they always go away. Are you still juggling the Jitters?" Papa asks.
"A bit," I say.
"What would you like to do about it?" Papa asks.

"I know! Let's silly-dance and sing those Jitters away," I say.

Jabbery, Mumblie, Jumblie!

The Jitters laugh too. When the Jitters laugh they float up to the ceiling like balloons.

"Oh, Papa, I wish there were no
Jitters to juggle anywhere tonight."
The Jitters turn into Glitters and burst
into stars.

They shoot out the window to help all my friends juggling the Jitters.

And they flitter and glitter until there are no more Jitters in the whole world, just starry-eyed children.

Papa tucks me into bed.
"Good night, Jacob."
"Good night, Papa."

And I go off to sleep.

Deborah Fannie Miller's poetry has been heard on CBC Radio, the Women's Television Network, and Vision TV. Her poems are in two anthologies and she's had three books of poetry published. *Grappling with the Grumblies*, her first children's book, won "The Steffie Young Readers' Choice Award." *Juggling the Jitters* is the second book in her "dealing with feelings" series. When Deborah gets the jitters, she likes to silly-dance to the Black Eyed Peas singing "I Gotta Feeling."

Visit Deborah at www.deborahfanniemiller.com

Danielle is a graduate of the Alberta College of Art and Design VCD program. She resides in Calgary and eats plants. She loves going to the zoo and making faces with all the animals.

Visit Danielle at www.daniellebazinet.com